# DISNEY
# ENCANTO

pi
kids®

An imprint of PHOENIX International Publications, Inc.

Chicago • London • New York • Hamburg • Mexico City • Sydney

Mirabel's family uses their magical gifts to help everyone in the Encanto. Isabela creates flowers, Luisa moves heavy objects, Julieta cooks healing food, Tía Pepa affects the weather, Dolores has super hearing, and Camilo can shape-shift. Only Mirabel didn't get a magical gift.

Look for Mirabel and her helpful Madrigal family:

Mirabel    Isabela    Luisa    Pepa    Dolores    Julieta    Camilo

Tonight is Antonio's magical-gift-reveal ceremony. Julieta prepares a feast. Casita, the magical house, decorates...itself! When Mirabel tries to help, Abuela Alma reminds her to be careful. The entire town relies on the family and their powerful gifts, so everything must be perfect.

Search for these fun and festive party supplies:

balero  pinwheels  party hats  woven bowl  yucca  coconut

At last, the family has a new gift—Antonio can communicate with animals! Rainforest friends race to join the party as everyone celebrates. Everyone but Mirabel. She leaves the party and discovers that Casita is cracking and falling apart!

As Mirabel warns her family, find Antonio's new animal friends:

jaguar

Chispi
the chigüiro

hummingbird

South American
tapir

boa constrictor

toucan

Before Mirabel can show anyone the cracks, they disappear! But Mirabel is sure that something is wrong. Luisa admits that she has been feeling...weaker. She wishes she could relax, but she feels too much pressure to always be strong.

Find these symbols of the pressure Luisa feels:

Casita    boulder    ship    sword    coffee bean    Luisa's door

Before he disappeared, Tío Bruno had visions. Pepa and Félix tell Mirabel that Bruno ruined their wedding day by predicting rain. Almost everyone in the Encanto was worried about Bruno's visions. Félix warns Mirabel that the last vision Bruno had was about her!

**Search for these people with stories to tell about Bruno:**

goldfish owner    Félix    Dolores    village priest    Isabela    villager

Mirabel finds Bruno! He's been hiding inside the walls—he can't bear to leave his family. Bruno reveals his last vision showed that the magic was in danger, and Mirabel has to save it! And now Bruno has a new vision that shows Mirabel must hug her sister Isabela.

Look for Bruno and the broken pieces of his vision:

When Mirabel visits Isabela, they argue. Isabela confesses she hates having to be perfect, which reveals a new ability—growing amazing new types of plants! Abuela Alma is upset with Mirabel for encouraging changes. As Mirabel expresses her sadness and anger, the Casita begins to crumble.

Before the house falls, find these "perfect" plants of Isabela's past:

flower couch   flower chair   flower Isabla   potted flowers   flower swan   flower tree

Abuela Alma and Mirabel come to an understanding, and are stronger for it! They welcome Bruno back with open arms and open minds. Everyone in the Encanto helps the Madrigals rebuild Casita. Mirabel adds her special doorknob to the front, and the magic is restored!

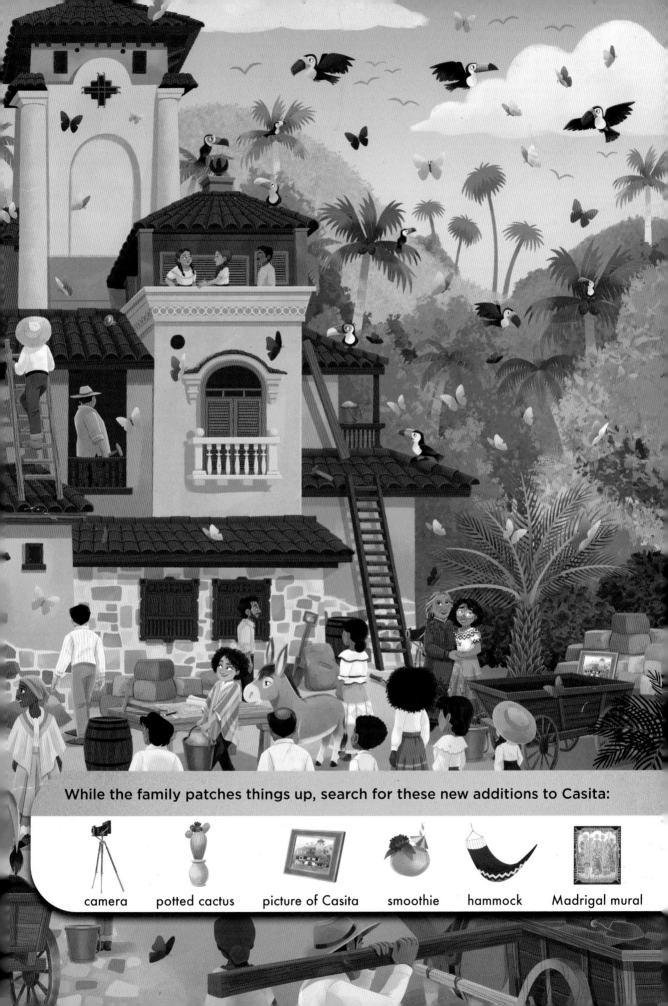

While the family patches things up, search for these new additions to Casita:

camera    potted cactus    picture of Casita    smoothie    hammock    Madrigal mural

## Go back to the Encanto and look for these curious community members:

## Snack your way back to the kitchen and find these things:

arepa con queso    bowl    pitcher    stack of plates    pot    salt container

## Boogie back to the party and search for these 6 guests:

## Fly back to Luisa's fantasy and pick up these pals:

## Blow back to the square and look for these signs of Pepa's moods:

lightning bolt    tornado       sun        rainbow     rain cloud     snowflake

## Scurry back to Bruno's place and find these furry friends:

## *Grow* back to Isabela's room and pick out these pretty plants:

cactus

sundew

bromeliad

cactus

blooming cactus    succulent

## Race back to the rebuilding and help find these useful tools:

doorknob

bucket of sand

hammer

shovel

trowel

architecture plans

## Ready for more magic? Float back to the beginning and find 25 yellow butterflies hidden throughout the book!